Bright**Summaries**.com

Northern Lights

by Philip Pullman

Northern Lights

BY PHILIP PULLMAN

PHILIP PULLMAN — 5

English writer — 5

NORTHERN LIGHTS
(HIS DARK MATERIALS – BOOK 1) — 7

First part of an initiation trilogy — 7

SUMMARY — 8

CHARACTER STUDY — 15

Lyra Belacqua (Lyra Silvertongue) — 15

Lord Asriel — 17

Marisa Coulter — 19

Iorek Byrnison — 20

Iofur Raknison — 20

The Gypsies — 21

Serafina Ladakka — 21

KEYS TO READING — 23

At the crossroads of genres — 23

The narrative scheme — 26

The Actancial Scheme — 29

The religious-political question: a heretical novel? — 30

AVENUES FOR REFLECTION — 35

A few questions for further reflection... — 35

TO GO FURTHER — 36

Reference edition — 36

Benchmark studies — 36

Adaptations — 36

PHILIP PULLMAN

ENGLISH WRITER

- **Born in 1946 in Norwich, England**
- **Some of his works:**
  - *The Subtle Knife (His Dark Materials – Volume 2)* (2000), novel
  - *The Amber Spyglass (His Dark Materials – Volume 3)* (2001), novel
  - *La Belle Sauvage* (2017), novel

Philip Pullman's father, a Royal Air Force pilot, was posted to Africa when the writer was a child. The family spent a few years there, but when his father died, his mother decided to return to England. Philip is marked by the figure of his grandfather, an Anglican clergyman, a great storyteller to whom he owes his taste for narration.

He studied philology at Oxford University. From the 1970s he began teaching and writing plays for his students, and in the 1980s was awarded a professorship at Oxford and Westminster. After the publication of *The Curse of the Ruby* (1986), he turned his attention to writing.

Passionate about stories, he writes mainly (but not exclusively) for young people, but does not consider himself a "writer": this term seems inappropriate to him, so he says he "writes stories" (presentation of the author, p. 503).

He is now one of the most widely read children's authors in the world.

NORTHERN LIGHTS (HIS DARK MATERIALS – BOOK 1)

FIRST PART OF AN INITIATION TRILOGY

- **Genre:** novel
- **Reference edition:** *Les Royaumes du Nord. À la croisée des mondes (tome 1)*, translated from English by Jean Esch, Paris, Gallimard Jeunesse, 2007, 500 p.
- **1st edition:** 1995
- **Themes:** Fantasy, initiation novel, magic, adolescence, steampunk, parallel worlds

Northern Lights (titled *The Golden Compass* in some countries) is the first volume of the *His Dark Materials* trilogy. It is a novel of initiation and is part of the youth fantasy trend.

It follows the adventures of Lyra, an eleven-year-old girl who sets out for the far north to rescue her friend Roger, who has been kidnapped by the mysterious Gobblers. It is set in "a world similar to our own – but different in many ways." (p. 7)

The book, although criticised at the time of its release by conservative Catholic circles, was a great success. Translated into 40 languages, with nearly 20 million copies sold, it is the second biggest success of the children's fantasy genre, after the *Harry Potter* saga.

Northern Lights has been adapted for film (*The Golden Compass*, 2007), theatre, radio, comics and video games.

SUMMARY

The story begins in England, at a time that may correspond to the second half of the 19th century (Victorian era). Eleven-year-old Lyra, a fair-haired, fearless girl with little interest in cleanliness, grows up in the city of Oxford at Jordan College, where she is taught, rather than raised, by the Scholars, a brotherhood of theologians. They, and in particular the Master, are responsible for the girl's education, as her parents are said to have died in an air crash. Lyra discovers the truth later: thirsting for power and recognition, they have preferred to abandon their daughter in favour of their own interests.

Lyra is always accompanied by Pantalaimon, her dæmon: in Pullman's world, every human being is linked to an animal that follows him everywhere and can change form according to the circumstances. With Roger the kitchen boy, her best friend, she is one of the only children living in the establishment. Not very obedient, she spends her time wandering around the city with her gang of friends. But mysterious child kidnappers, known as the Gobblers, are rampant in the region and the number of disappearances is increasing. One day, it is Roger's turn to be kidnapped.

Hidden in a cupboard during a council of scholars, Lyra witnesses the presentation of Lord Asriel, a great explorer returning from a mission in the North. He is introduced as her uncle, but turns out to be her father. He tells his colleagues about his discoveries on Dust, a mysterious particle, as well as a photograph of the Aurora, a celestial phenomenon which makes it possible to see a city located in another world.

Mrs Coulter, an explorer and head of the General Oblation Board, is visiting Jordan College. She insists on hiring Lyra as her assistant and taking her to London. The child is charmed, looking forward to seeing the world. And she already knows that London is just one stop on her journey north to rescue Roger. Before leaving, the Master has given her the alethiometer, a magical object, a kind of compass with symbols which, as its name suggests (*alethia*: truth; *metre*: measure), enables her to read the truth. An interrupted sentence, in which the Master refers to Lord Asriel, will haunt Lyra throughout the novel. She interprets these words as a mission: to give the alethiometer to her father.

After some time spent idealising the beautiful and powerful Mrs Coulter (who, she later learns, is in fact her mother), Lyra discovers darker sides to her protector and begins to distrust her: she is in fact the head of the Gobblers (the General Oblation Board, which we will discuss in detail later).

During a party organised by the General Oblation Board, the young girl overhears a conversation between the guests: Lord Asriel is said to be held prisoner in Svalbard, in the North, by the panserbjornes, armoured bears reputed to be invincible. Increasingly suspicious of

Mrs Coulter (the heroine later learns that her mother is behind Lord Asriel's captivity, among other plots), Lyra decides to flee.

She is immediately pursued and rescued by three gypsies, who take her into their community. Ma Costa takes care of her as if she were her own daughter, and for good reason, she was her wet nurse when the young heroine was abandoned by her mother.

They reach Fens, where a large gathering of thousands of gypsies is being held to organise an expedition north to find the children kidnapped by the Gobblers. Outside, a manhunt is on to find Lyra. The gypsies hide her and the expedition sets off for the North. Lyra discovers her navigational skills. Farder Coram and John Faa, the gypsy leader, reveal to her who her real parents are.

The convoy arrives in the town of Trollesund in Lapland. Lyra, Farder Coram and John Faa meet the consul Lanselius, who tells them where the witch Serafina Ladakka is, who can help them in their quest, as she is in debt to Farder Coram. The consul also explains that an organisation called the Northern Exploration Company, under the pretext of searching for minerals, is in fact controlled by the General Oblation Board. This company captures children and holds them prisoner in order to practice "intercision": a process that separates the children from their dæmons.

The consul also puts them on the trail of Iorek Byrnison, an exiled bear who has had his armour stolen. When

Lyra finds Iorek's armour, he regains his dignity and agrees to accompany them to protect them.

The caravan heads back north. The witch Serafina Ladakka's goose dæmon tells Lyra that the Dust seekers are operating in an Experimental Station in Bolvangar ("the Evil Fields").

Lyra, increasingly at ease with the alethiometer, consults it: it tells her that not far from the caravan's route there is a village haunted by the ghost of a child. She sets off with Iorek for the village, where she finds Toni, a little boy curled up, deprived of his dæmon. He is said to be "mutilated": a victim of intercision, he has been separated from his dæmon. She takes him back to the caravan, but he dies in the night.

The Samoyeds attack the caravan and Lyra is captured. The Samoyeds hand her over to the Bastards. She is taken to the Bolvangar Experimental Station where she is reunited with Roger.

Trapped in Bolvangar, Lyra enters a room where she discovers dæmons locked in glass cages. With the help of the goose, the dæmon of the witch Serafina Ladakka, she manages to free them. Mrs Coulter arrives in Bolvangar in her zeppelin. Lyra sneaks into the ceilings to spy on a meeting: the Station's leaders discuss a new technique for separating dæmons and children: the guillotine. Lyra is spotted and taken away to be separated from Pantalaimon. The guillotine is ready to separate them when Mrs Coulter intervenes to stop the process.

Mrs Coulter wants to get hold of the alethiometer. Lyra then gives her a box made by Iorek, in which a spy-fly was imprisoned, and it swoops down on Mrs Coulter's dæmon. The latter being destabilised (the contacts on a dæmon being felt physically by its human), Lyra takes advantage of this to escape and set off the fire alarm, having observed during a simulation the very poor organisation of the staff. All the children escape from the Station. Walking at night, in the snow, they are caught by the Tartars, nomadic warriors living in the North, who are themselves immediately attacked by the witches and by Iorek. Then Lee Scoresby, an aeronaut and friend of the bear, comes to rescue them in a balloon. After a battle involving Tartars, gypsies, witches and the Inferno, Lyra flees with Roger and Iorek in the airship.

They fly north, pulled by Serafina Ladakka, towards Svalbard, the fortress of the panserbjornes, which is considered impregnable. But a storm hits and Lyra is thrown out of the balloon. She is captured by bears in armour and imprisoned in the fortress.

Locked up in a dungeon, she asks to see Iofur Raknison, the bear king, who agrees to meet her. Iofur, sitting on his throne with a large rag doll on his lap, dreams of being a man and having a dæmon. Lyra tells him that she herself is Iorek Byrnison's dæmon and that she wants to become the king's dæmon. The only way to become one would be for him to kill Iorek in a single combat. In this way she saves Iorek from being killed by the army of bears. The bears, seeing him coming, will let him enter the palace to fight Iofur.

Iorek is seen in the distance by the sentries. Lyra asks to join him to tell him that he will have to fight against Iofur. He thanks her, as he has been dreaming of this confrontation for a long time, and nicknames her Lyra Silvertongue. After a violent fight, Iorek kills Iofur and becomes king of the bears.

Lyra, accompanied by Roger, Iorek, and a few other bears, sets out to find Lord Asriel, who is being held prisoner on top of a cliff in a luxurious house. As a prisoner considered political, he is given all the care he requires. Lyra enters the house with Roger and Iorek, with the intention of handing the alethiometer to Lord Asriel. The latter, thinking himself unable to use the object without the manual, leaves it to Lyra (who knows how to use it by intuition alone).

Lord Asriel abducts Roger: he needs the energy that spreads during the separation of the child from his dæmon to be able to create a bridge to the other world, the one seen through the Dawn.

Lyra and Iorek go in pursuit of Lord Asriel. They are attacked by witches and then caught by Mrs Coulter. The bears take care of fighting Mrs Coulter, accompanied by the Tartars. Lyra continues her pursuit with Iorek. Their run is interrupted by a crevasse, which can only be crossed by a fragile bridge. Iorek is too heavy and has to give up the chase. Lyra continues alone. She joins Lord Asriel, who is preparing the separation of

Roger and his dæmon. Roger dies. Lord Asriel and Mrs Coulter, who has joined them, kiss like two lovers. Mrs Coulter refuses to follow Lord Asriel who escapes to the other world. Lyra decides to follow him to enter the sky of Dawn…

CHARACTER STUDY

LYRA BELACQUA (LYRA SILVERTONGUE)

Lyra is a young blonde girl with clear eyes. She is slender and small for her age. Her hair and nails are often dirty.

In *Northern Lights*, the passages that tell of Lyra's adventures are in internal focus. The reader follows her progress through the eyes of the child. But the narrator alternates points of view, introducing passages in zero focus to give the reader information of which Lyra is unaware and which heightens the dramatic tension. For example, a discussion between the Master and the Librarian, from which Lyra is absent, tells us that her role in the future of the world is crucial, but that she must not be aware of it (p. 47).

Her surname, Belacqua, refers to a character in Dante's *Divine Comedy*: in the Italian poet, Belacqua is one of the "indolent", those souls who are unable to choose and act between good and evil.

Lyra is the daughter of an adulterous relationship between Marisa Coulter (Mrs Coulter) and Lord Asriel. When she was born, she had to be hidden by her mother because Mrs Coulter's husband, faced with the child's obvious resemblance to her biological father, tried to eliminate her. Lord Asriel, refusing to entrust her to the convent, entrusts the Scholars of the College with her education.

Undisciplined, she spends her time playing with children in the street, especially with Roger Parslow, the kitchen boy from Jordan College. She has little interest in the theoretical knowledge dispensed by the Scholars, but her relationship to knowledge is complex: for her curiosity about Dust and the other world will lead her to cross the Dawn, where many other dangers await her in the rest of the book.

She is also very cunning: an expert in the art of lying, she will develop extraordinary faculties of intuition, notably in her use of the alethiometer. Carried by her courage, she represents, within this totalitarian system, the revolutionary impulse, supported by the aspiration to freedom.

Dæmons In the world of Lyra, every human being has a dæmon. Taking the form of an animal, it changes its appearance according to the situation. When he reaches adulthood, his form becomes permanent.

Between outside and inside, between the other and oneself, the dæmon is like an extension of the character. The communication between the human and his dæmon can be verbal or infraverbal (for example, he becomes very small when the character is afraid; or, in the other direction, the human feels touched when his dæmon is touched by someone). With the exception of witches, humans and dæmons cannot move away from each other. They are bound together by a bond so strong that the threat of being separated plunges them into deep distress.

A law, "the great taboo", forbids touching the dæmon of another human. When Lyra, in Bolvangar, has Pantalaimon snatched away from her by the Inferno, she feels this aggression as if "a foreign hand had entered her" (p. 350).

The General Oblation Board's plan is to separate the children from their dæmons, because once they are "mutilated" they are like ghosts and no longer represent a danger to the Magisterium.

Pantalaimon

Pantalaimon (whom Lyra calls "Pan") is the heroine's dæmon. His name is based on the Greek words *Pan* ("all") and *eleimon* ("merciful"): he is the one who forgives all. Sometimes in the form of an ermine to keep her warm, sometimes a mouse to remain discreet by slipping into her pocket, sometimes a cat or a bird, he is her most faithful companion. He is so inseparable from her that it is difficult to give him a character status as such.

LORD ASRIEL

Lord Asriel is a tall, beastly-looking man with broad shoulders and a "dark and fierce" face (p. 23). He exudes such strength that no one can patronise him (p. 24).

Lord Asriel, Lyra's father, first introduced as her uncle, is a scholar at Jordan College. A solitary and mysterious figure, he is a great explorer and leads expeditions to the North. To finance a new journey, he tells the Scholars of Jordan College about his discoveries on the Dust. His project is to establish a bridge to access this city visible only during the Aurora: a parallel universe, superimposed on ours (in the northern lights, the electric particles of the Aurora make the matter of our world finer, and allow us to see other universes.) His megalomaniacal spiritual quest leads him in the footsteps of "the origin of Dust, of death, of sin, of misery, of the taste for destruction". He says he wants to "kill death." (p. 475).

At the beginning of the book, the Master of Jordan College tries to poison him. This episode sets us on the wrong track: as a potential victim, our sympathy naturally turns to him. But he turns out to be selfish and ruthless, including killing Lyra's best friend Roger.

A stern and powerful character, he exerts a fascination on his daughter, who bears the brunt of his selfishness. She says she doesn't love him, yet she can't stop admiring him, and when she learns that he is imprisoned in Svalbard, the impregnable fortress, she will do anything to find him.

Although he only appears at the beginning and end of the novel, Lord Asriel is a central character, as is his fascination for Lyra. He is the subject of conversations between the protagonists, and above all, it is he who stirs Lyra's desire to know more about the Dust, and it is towards him that the heroine's quest tends.

His dæmon is a leopard, "proud, beautiful and murderous" (p. 475).

MARISA COULTER

Mrs Coulter is described as a slim, beautiful young woman with shiny black hair.

She is a character who serves several functions. At the beginning of the book, Lyra, having lived at Jordan College only with dull and austere older men, has great admiration for this woman who has come from London to look for her. She sees her as the mother she would have liked to have – and who turns out to be her real mother. Mrs Coulter helps to launch Lyra's journey.

Like her ambivalent relationship with Lord Asriel, whom she has imprisoned but who appears to be the only man she can love, Mrs Coulter knows how to use her charms to achieve her intentions. Power-hungry, she will do anything to dominate. First married to Edward Coulter, an ambitious politician, she directs all her energy to her ambition after his death: she chairs the General Oblation Board. It is this second, darker side that will dominate the character from now on. She foments various plots: for example, she is behind the exile of Iorek Byrnison, so that Iofur Raknison will reign over the bears; she is at the head of the project to separate the children from their dæmon; and she has had Lord Asriel, her lover, imprisoned. With Lyra, she is not so cruel, but seems to have some dark agenda.

Her dæmon is a golden-furred monkey, which she uses to capture children, among other things.

IOREK BYRNISON

Iorek Byrnison, a prince banished from the kingdom of Svalbard for having killed one of his fellow creatures, is a pansebjorne, a bear in armour with colossal strength. The armour of bears is comparable to the dæmon of humans: it constitutes their spiritual essence. A bear without armour (as is the case with Iorek when Lyra meets him) is a depressed bear, without a soul. Lyra allows him to find it, in exchange for which Iorek will follow the girl throughout her adventures. His armour is rusty and dented, but fits him perfectly, in contrast to the beautiful armour of the bears of the kingdom, and particularly that of Iofur Raknison, his rival and king of Svalbard, whom he kills in an organised fight after which he takes his place.

A warrior and blacksmith, but also very cunning (it is said that no one can fool a bear), Iorek helps Lyra to overcome many obstacles and saves her on several occasions.

IOFUR RAKNISON

Iofur Raknison is the king of the bears in armour of Svalbard. His armour is luxurious, but he "dreams of another soul" (p. 440): his greatest wish is to possess a dæmon. Since animals do not have one, he has made a rag doll in the shape of a man to make up for this lack. The contrast between a royal bear in shining armour and the doll he is holding is singular. It evokes one of the main issues of the book (and of adolescence), namely the non-linear transition from childhood to adulthood (the individual "in passage" combines childhood codes with others borrowed from adulthood).

Iofur, wanting to possess a dæmon, already functions as a human being. For this reason, he is, unlike his fellow dæmon, vulnerable to deception. Lyra will take advantage of this to have him beaten by Iorek.

THE GYPSIES

Ma Costa, Farder Coram, John Faa, are the gypsies who take Lyra in and protect her from the manhunt organised by the General Oblation Board. Their community has lost many children to the kidnappers. They are an essential aid to Lyra in her quest to the North. They reveal a lot of information to Lyra about her past, especially about her parents.

SERAFINA LADAKKA

Although it is difficult to categorise them – some in the role of helpers, others in the role of opponents – witches are not equated with ugly old women in this novel. They can be beautiful and still be young, even though they may live for hundreds of years. Serafina Ladakka is an example. This beautiful green-eyed woman appears more as a wise and benevolent figure than as the archetypal witch that fairy tales have left us. Witches move in the polar cold on fir branches, covered with a simple silk veil. They feel the cold, but can bear it, which makes them more human.

Serafina Ladakka helps Lyra, but it is mainly her goose-dæmon (because, unlike humans, witches can walk away from it) that reveals essential information, such as the location of the Experimental Station.

KEYS TO READING

AT THE CROSSROADS OF GENRES

A fantasy novel

The story takes place in a world that has many similarities with our own (notably the geography and the setting of Victorian England). However, many elements of the marvellous are present from the beginning of the book (including the presence of dæmons); and as the story progresses, these elements will become more and more present (imaginary creatures, witches, etc.).

Northern Lights can be classified in the protean genre of fantasy: supernatural elements and magic are an integral part of the characters' world (as opposed to the fantasy genre, where the supernatural, by breaking into the "real" world, causes anxiety).

Subcategories of fantasy books

The classification of fantasy works can be specified according to various criteria. One of these is the nature of the space-time setting, which is particularly relevant in the case of the *Northern Lights*. Marshall et al. in *Fantasy Literature* (1979) distinguish between **high** and **low fantasy**.

In **high fantasy**, the characters live exclusively in an imaginary world with its own history, geography and laws. The atmosphere is often fairytale-like (e.g. *The Lord of the Rings*).

Low Fantasy is the term used to describe works in which the plot takes place in a world close to the real world and communicates with another world, notably through passages from which there is sometimes no return.

Northern Lights is therefore part of low fantasy: Lyra's world, although incorporating supernatural elements (such as ambaric energy, dæmons, etc.), has great similarities with our own: she grows up in Oxford, spends some time in a London that could be that of the Victorian era, before travelling to Lapland (the Great North). The supernatural elements are therefore slipped in "naturally" in a setting that is not immediately at odds with our world. As far as the time frame is concerned, there is no precise information that allows us to date the period in which the story takes place.

Alongside the plot, the existence of another world, visible only from the far north, during the Aurora (Northern Lights), is revealed: a city that Lyra will reach at the very end of the novel.

Steampunk

The book also borrows from the *steampunk* aesthetic (especially in the first part, which takes place in England).

Steampunk (literally "steam punk") is a literary and cinematographic trend that is usually set in England at the end of the 19th century, the time of the first industrial revolution. It is a type of uchrony (a literary narrative whose premise is the rewriting of history: the historical setting is that of the real world, but an event differs from it and leads to a series of fictional consequences). *Steampunk* is set in a world where steam engines and mechanisms made of noble metals (such as copper or brass) are very present. Stephen Norrington's *The League of Extraordinary Gentlemen* (2003), a film adaptation of Alan Moore's comic book, is an emblematic work of this movement.

The space-time setting of *Northern Lights is* reminiscent of Victorian England (style of dress of the characters, car-free Oxford street, horse fair, etc.). Certain objects, notably the alethiometer, which looks like a large copper and crystal compass, refer to these imaginary tools with apparent mechanics, which are very present in the *steampunk* universe. Although steam engines proper are absent from the book, Mrs Coulter's zeppelin and Lee Scoresby's balloon are recurrent elements in this universe.

An initiation story

Moreover, *Northern Lights* (and even more so the trilogy as a whole) is an initiation story – a narrative structure frequently found in fantasy books. At the beginning of the book, Lyra is still a child. She is only thinking of playing, of defying the limits of a paternalistic authority represented by the Scholars (these "fathers" who seem too old to be really interested in the education of the intrepid young girl: the conflict of generations being exacerbated, they cannot understand her). Over the course of the novel, and even more so over the course of the trilogy, she is confronted with a series of obstacles that make her suffer and evolve. She refines her art of cunning and lying, which is no longer only intended to justify her disciplinary misdeeds to the scholars as at the beginning of the book, but allows her to develop plans to save lives. She also develops extraordinary powers of intuition through the reading of the alethiometer.

Despite the obstacles, she does not back down, as if called by her destiny. She will be confronted with the harsh reality she was protected from at Jordan College: the truth about her parents and the fate of abducted children, the ruthlessness of some adults' lust for power, their cruelty. As she goes through these trials, she broadens her view of the world. She will emerge less naive. At the end of the third volume, Pantalaimon will take its final form, a sign that the heroine is entering adulthood.

THE NARRATIVE SCHEME

Northern Lights follows a relatively classic narrative pattern in the genre of the initiation novel.

Initial situation

With her best friend Roger, Lyra wanders the city of Oxford, looking for opportunities to break the rules of the austere scholars of Jordan College. In and around the city, the Inferno are a mysterious group that is the stuff of legend, as they abduct children. One night, hidden in a wardrobe, Lyra attends a meeting where she learns about the existence of Dust, a particle visible only from the far north. She wants to follow her uncle Lord Asriel who is going back, but he refuses to take her.

Disruptive elements

Roger is abducted by the Infernos. This element initiates Lyra's quest to find her friend, but acts more as a narrative lever that will lead her to the discovery of the object of her true quest: finding Lord Asriel.

Events

- Mrs Coulter appears. Lyra accompanies her to London and becomes her assistant.

- Lyra decides to run away from Mrs Coulter's house. Chased, she is saved by the gypsies. Lyra embarks with them towards the North.

- Lyra meets Iorek Byrnison, a bear deprived of his armour, which the girl finds. Iorek now accompanies her.

- The gypsy caravan is attacked and Lyra is captured by Samoyeds who sell her to the Bastards. She ends up in Bolvangar, the Experimental Station, where she meets Roger again.

- She managed to escape.

- Lyra is taken in by Lee Scoresby. They fly to Svalbard.

- An attack by cliff monsters causes Lyra to fall off the ball. She is captured by the armoured bears and taken to Svalbard.

- She is taken prisoner in the bear kingdom.

- She manages to arrange a fight between King Iofur and Iorek, Lyra's companion, who wins the fight.

Resolution

After defeating Iofur, Iorek becomes King of Svalbard. He accompanies Lyra to deliver Lord Asriel, who surprisingly is not happy to be freed. The latter does not want the Aletheometer.

Final situation

Lord Asriel escapes by kidnapping Roger, whom he kills so that he can use an installation of philosophical tools to build a bridge to the other world. Lyra, now alone, follows her father to the other side of the Dawn.

In freeing Lord Asriel, Lyra, although she achieves the object of her quest, seems to make a mistake. Indeed, her father, once freed, rushes to kill Roger and flees through the Aurora to the other world. But this twist (apparently a failure for Lyra) will allow the heroine to discover the other world, which will be the subject of the second volume of the trilogy.

THE ACTANCIAL SCHEME

As the actancial scheme is action-based, we will take Lyra's quest to free Lord Asriel from the realm of Svalbard as the main model – the search for Roger may be seen only as a step towards the reunion with the Scholar (indeed, Roger is an underdeveloped character). Although it precedes, in the chronology of the story, the quest to Svalbard, the search for the missing friend is secondary in terms of the plot.

- Fate: Lyra is destined to play a major role in the fate of the world (unconscious destiny of the main character, which is evoked by the Master)

- The Master, a "false" actant (Greimas): Lyra believes, as a result of an interrupted sentence, that she must hand over the alethiometer to Lord Asriel. The Master is therefore not "really" an actant, but Lyra imagines him as such.

- Lyra's personal desire to know more about her father (for reasons that may have more to do with what Lord Asriel knows and could teach her than with the emotional bond between the two protagonists)

- Lyra's curiosity for the Far North, Dust and Dawn.

Recipients

- Lord Asriel, who will be released

- Lyra, but who is immediately disappointed by her father

Additives

- Dr. Lanselius, who will give him valuable information

- Lyra's courage and cunning

- The gypsies, who take her in and take her north

- Iorek Byrnison, the bear who protects her with his strength

- The witch Serafina Ladakka and her goose dæmon

- Lee Scoresby saving her with his ball

- The alethiometer, which reveals the truth and allows her to deceive the king of Svalbard, among others

Opponents

- Mrs Coulter, who wants to hijack Lyra and use her as bait to capture other children

- The General Oblation Board, which removes Lyra

- The Tartars, who attack the gypsy convoy

- The bears in armour of Svalbard

THE RELIGIOUS-POLITICAL QUESTION: A HERETICAL NOVEL?

In the background of his trilogy, Philip Pullman elaborates an original "theology" that mixes philosophy,

Christianity, quantum physics and parallel universes. *Northern Lights* sets out the foundations of this "theology".

The controversy

When the film adaptation of the first volume (*The Golden Compass*) was released in the United States, conservative Christian circles (particularly *the Catholic League for Religious and Civic Rights*) protested, denouncing the film as heretical, which would sell "atheism to children" (Noiville, F. "Qualifié d'antichrétien, l'écrivain Philip Pullman préfère en rire", *Le Monde*, 3 December 2007)

Antoine Gallimard, Philip Pullman's French publisher, had this to say (*ibid.*):

> *"If there are metaphysical questions, they have nothing to do with the Gospels. They reflect a spiritual quest familiar to children. Who are we? Where do we come from? What is behind the visible world?*

So what was it that so disturbed Catholic circles?

Lyra's world is a dystopian world (a dystopia is a fictional story that is set in a totalitarian society, thus leaving little room for the individual). It is a critique of religious organisation. The order of society is governed by an all-powerful Church, with the Magisterium as its repressive organ. The repressive aspect of this totalitarian system is less about the behaviour of individuals than about a closed dogma that prevents any research, spiritual or scientific, that does not follow the imposed theological canons. Thought control is exercised with the aim of preserving a certain world order. The discovery of the Dust is a threat to the Church, and the institution tries to keep the existence of the mysterious particle and the parallel universes to which it is linked secret. In the world of Lyra, political organisation is therefore inseparable from religion. The *Magisterium* is an allegory of the power struggles, rivalry, secrets and treachery that are common in any political organisation, let *alone* the Church.

Moreover, Pullman, as he does with geography, hijacks history: he mixes the names of historical figures into his story, but reinvents them, thus blurring the boundaries between fiction and reality, giving his novel an uchronistic character. For example, he makes John Calvin, the great reformer, into a pope, who, after transferring the seat of the papacy to Geneva, is said to have set up the Consistorial Court, whose mission is to fight against heretics. From this (fictitious) moment on, the Church exercised absolute control over the world. After John Calvin's death, the various colleges, councils and universities came together to form the Magisterium, within which many disputes arose.

A rewriting of Original Sin

The General Oblation Board, known to the children as Gobblers, is an organ of the Magisterium. One of its aims is to separate children from their dæmon (in the manner of castrati singers in the sixteenth century, who were castrated so that they would not mutate): in this way, as they grow up, the children would not attract the Dust.

Why do the Gobblers practice such mutilation?

Pullman, in a rewriting of an Old Testament passage, has Lord Asriel say: "By the sweat of thy brow thou shalt eat thy bread, until thou return to the ground, for thou wast taken from it. For thou art dust, and unto dust shalt thou return" (p. 469). According to Lyra's father, the name "Dust" has a biblical origin. Pullman goes further in his adaptation of Genesis: he rewrites part of the myth of Adam and Eve, which ends as follows:

> *"But when the man and the woman knew their dæmons, they understood that a great change had taken place in them, for until then it was as if they were one with all the creatures of the earth and the air, and there was no difference between them.*
>
> *Then they saw this difference, they knew good and evil…" (p. 468)*

The challenge of "knowing one's dæmon" thus goes beyond the quality of the relationship between the human and his animal alter ego. This "great change" is the entry into adulthood (at which point, it should be remembered, the form of the dæmon becomes fixed, and the human being can therefore "know" it). From this "knowledge" (which, in Pullman's theology, *is* original sin) comes the reception of Dust (which is deposited only on "conscious" beings): the human being, on entering adulthood, becomes conscious, which for the General Oblation Board represents a threat.

Parallel worlds

In Lyra's world, the Church teaches that there are two worlds: the material world and the spiritual world (which is divided between Heaven and Hell). Once again, Pullman plays with the boundaries between fiction and reality, as this dichotomy could apply to the real Church. In the novel, Barnard and Stokes, two heretical theologians, hypothesise the existence of many worlds similar to Lyra's, "neither heaven nor hell, but material worlds, tainted by sin" (p. 46). This theory, refuted by the Church, would be supported by research in Experimental Theology, carried out by Lord Asriel among others. The Master, by attempting, at the beginning of the novel, to poison the explorer, seeks to protect the college from accusations of heresy that might call into question the support of their patrons (such as the General Oblation Board). Until Lord Asriel, no one thought it was possible to cross from one world to another. His research leads him to believe that it is possible, which the end of the book will confirm.

AVENUES FOR REFLECTION

A FEW QUESTIONS FOR FURTHER REFLECTION...

- What makes *Northern Lights* an initiation novel?

- How are parallel worlds a hope against totalitarianism?

- Make an actancial diagram of Iorek Byrnison in his conquest of the bear kingdom.

- How is the structure of the book similar to that of the story?

- Compare the film adaptation and the novel.

- Phillip Pullman does not consider himself a writer, but a storyteller. Explain.

- How does the author blur the lines between reality and fiction?

- How can we understand that the shape of the dæmons is fixed in adulthood?

TO GO FURTHER

REFERENCE EDITION

PULLMAN P., *Les Royaumes du Nord. À la croisée des mondes - tome 1*, Paris, Gallimard, 2007.

BENCHMARK STUDIES

BAZIN L. « Mondes possibles, lendemains qui chantent? Projections utopiques dans la littérature de jeunesse contemporaine », *TRANS* – [En ligne], 14 | 2012, online 24 July 2012, accessed 01 October 2016. URL: http://trans.revues.org/567 ; DOI : 10.4000/trans.567

HÉBERT L. , « Le modèle actanciel », in Louis Hébert (ed.), *Signo* [online], Rimouski (Québec), 2006

NOIVILLE F. « Qualifié d'antichrétien, l'écrivain Philip Pullman préfère en rire », *Le Monde* https://www.lemonde.fr/cinema/article/2007/12/03/qualifie-d-antichretien-l-ecrivain-philip-pullman-prefere-en-rire_985280_3476.html

ADAPTATIONS

Comics: MELCHIOR-DURAND S., OUBRERIE C., *Les Royaumes du Nord*, tome 1/3 Paris, Gallimard, 2014

Film adaptation: WEITZ C., *The Golden Compass*, 2007

Radio drama: British radio BBC Radio 4, 2003

Theatre: HYTNER N., *His Darkness Materials*, 2003

Video game: *Crossroads: The Golden Compass*, SEGA, 2008

Your opinion is important to us!
Leave a comment on the website of your online bookshop
and share your favourites on social networks!

Milton Keynes UK
Ingram Content Group UK Ltd.
UKHW022257060924
1537UKWH00023B/384